Dear Parent:

Psst . . . you're looking at the Super Secret Weapon of Reading. It's called comics.

STEP INTO READING® COMIC READERS are a perfect step in learning to read. They provide visual cues to the meaning of words and helpfully break out short pieces of dialogue into speech balloons.

Here are some terms commonly associated with comics:
   PANEL: A section of a comic with a box drawn around it.
   CAPTION: Narration that helps set the scene.
   SPEECH BALLOON: A bubble containing dialogue.
   GUTTER: The space between panels.

Tips for reading comics with your child:

• Have your child read the speech balloons while you read the captions.
• Ask your child: What is a character feeling? How can you tell?
• Have your child draw a comic showing what happens after the book is finished.

STEP INTO READING® COMIC READERS are designed to engage and to provide an empowering reading experience. They are also fun. The best-kept secret of comics is that they create lifelong readers. And that will make you the real hero of the story!

Jennifer L. Holm and Matthew Holm
Co-creators of the Babymouse and Squish series

For Ravi

DC COMICS™

Copyright © 2013 DC Comics.
DC SUPER FRIENDS and all related characters and elements
are trademarks of and © DC Comics.
WB SHIELD: ™ & © Warner Bros. Entertainment Inc.
(s13)

RHUS29255

All rights reserved. Published in the United States by Random House Children's Books, a division
of Random House, Inc., 1745 Broadway, New York, NY 10019, and in Canada by Random House
of Canada Limited, Toronto.

Step into Reading, Random House, and the Random House colophon are registered trademarks
of Random House, Inc.

Visit us on the Web!
StepIntoReading.com
randomhouse.com/kids
dckids.kidswb.com

Educators and librarians, for a variety of teaching tools, visit us at RHTeachersLibrarians.com

ISBN 978-0-449-81616-5 (trade) – ISBN 978-0-449-81617-2 (lib. bdg.) –
ISBN 978-0-449-81618-9 (ebook)
Printed in the United States of America
10 9 8 7 6 5 4 3 2 1

A COMIC READER

CATCH CATWOMAN!

By Billy Wrecks

Illustrated by Erik Doescher, Mike DeCarlo,
and David Tanguay

Random House 🏠 New York

It's a quiet night in Gotham City.

Hawkman flies
to the rescue.

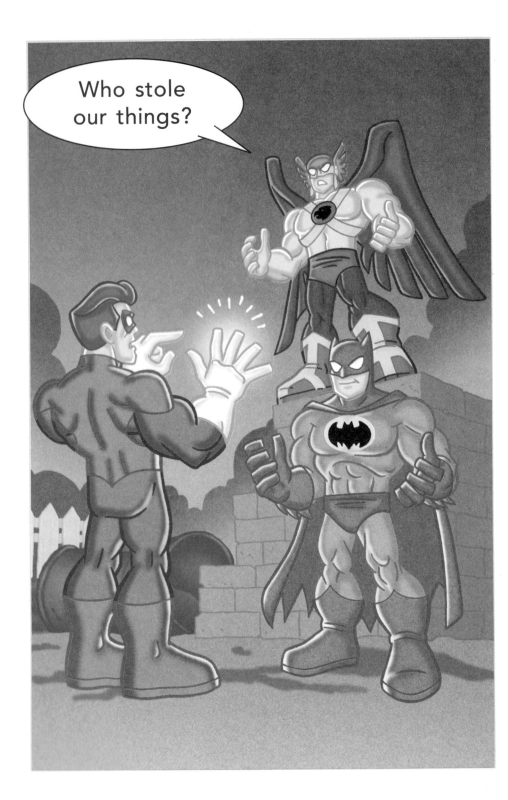

Pointed ears.	Claws.

Black suit.	Batman knows!

Catwoman!

15

Catwoman sneaks into the cat show.

The Blue Tiger
is one of a kind.

18

Catwoman uses Batman's Utility Belt to stop the guards.

Batarangs!

Bat-Cuffs!

Batrope!

Catwoman smashes the moat wall with Hawkman's mace.

Catwoman crashes through a wall.

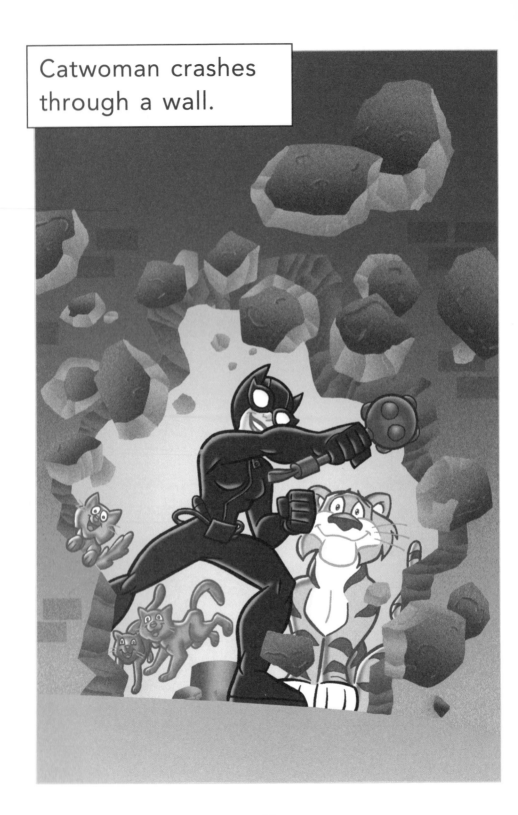

She plans to use Green Lantern's ring.

Let's fly!

The power ring sparks and sputters!

The Blue Tiger pounces.

The Super Friends
return the Blue Tiger.

Time to go.

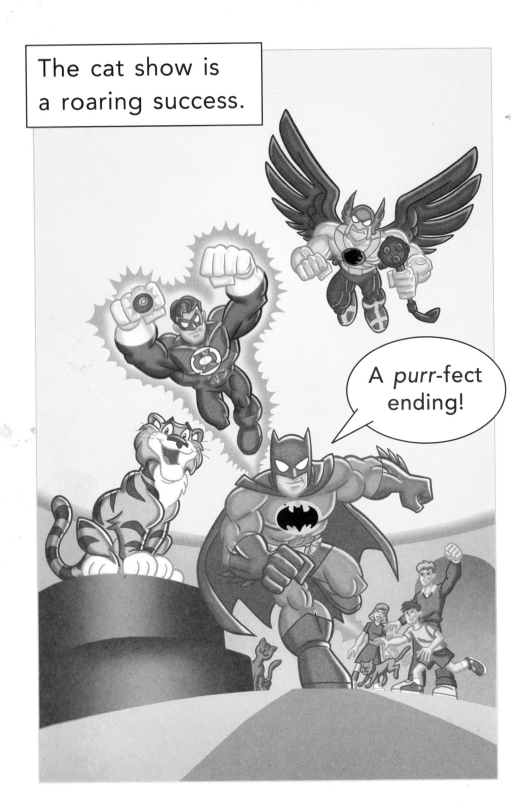